Susan Snyder

There's a Frog Trapped in the Bathroom

McCabe Children's Press

ISBN 0-9715411-0-8

This story is dedicated

to all my family

and friends who believed in me

and pushed me to succeed...

Thank you!

There's a frog
trapped
in the
bathroom!!
The girls began
to shout.
They nearly
knocked
each other
down,
As they
scrambled
to get out!

There's a frog
trapped
in the bathroom
You all just come
and see
Please SOMEONE
try to catch him...
Before he jumps
on me!

There's a frog
trapped
in the bathroom!
And we don't
know
what to do!
If you try
to go around
him,
He may just
jump on you!

There's a frog trapped in the bathroom!

Now we don't know what to think!

When we peeked around the corner,

He was swimming in the sink!

There's a frog
trapped
in the bathroom!
Now he's climbing
up the wall!
I'm afraid to try
to pass him…
Because he just
may fall!

There's a frog
trapped
in the bathroom!
I think he likes
it there...
Because everyone
is screaming,
And he doesn't
seem to care!!

There's a frog trapped
in the bathroom!
HE thinks he looks
quite charming.
He doesn't seem
to understand…
What the girls find
so alarming!

The frog just left
the bathroom!
He came out and
hopped away!
I guess he just
got bored,
And decided
not to stay!

anna johanson

Once the frog

had left

the bathroom,

The children

all stopped

squealing.

I guess no

one yet had

noticed...

THAT BIG SPIDER ON THE CEILING!!

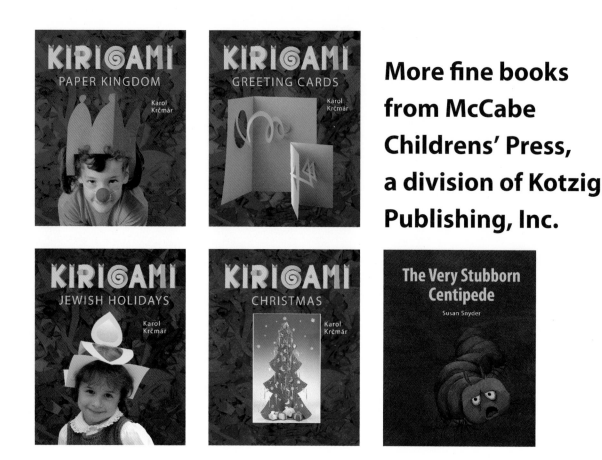

More fine books from McCabe Childrens' Press, a division of Kotzig Publishing, Inc.

Susan Snyder

There's a Frog Trapped in the Bathroom

Graphic design and Typography: Radoslav Tokoš
Illustration: Anna Johanson
Editor: Susan McCabe
Published by McCabe Children's Press
A division of Kotzig Publishing, Inc.
Printed in Slovakia
24 pages, 1st edition

www.kotzigpublishing.com

ISBN 0-9715411-0-8